This book belongs to:

_____

Dedication

This book is dedicated to uprooted people from every place and time, whose spirits have proven that after adversity, life goes on.

And sometimes, there is even dancing.

Fiddles & Spoons

Journey of an Acadian Mouse

Written by Lila Hope-Simpson
Illustrated by Doretta Groenendyk

DPG
Dery Publishing Group

Montréal
2004

It was fiddle night in the Dubois household, and under the floorboards, the mice were bursting with excitement!

Cecile Souris wore her linen dress, dyed a bright beet-root red, and her tail twitched with anticipation. On Saturday night, when the floorboards started to beat to the rhythm of the music and spoons and dancing upstairs, Cecile would grab her little brother Etienne and, together, they would dance until the moon lay low in the Grand Pré sky.

The best part of the musical nights was the food. On most nights, the mouse family would scrounge for crumbs of flaxseeds, grains, and vegetable peelings, but on Saturday nights, when the Dubois family gathered around the kitchen table with their fiddles and spoons, the aromas were delicious! There would be freshly-baked corn bread, chicken fricot and meat pie, with apple tarts or molasses taffy for dessert. And sometimes there would even be cheese! The Souris family would wait for the crumbs to fall between the floorboards, then eat until they had their fill.

Papa Souris worked hard all week in the fields, gathering seeds, nuts and kernels, and come Saturday night, he too was ready to indulge in the music and the foot-stomping merriment of the Dubois household. Mama Souris would take off her burlap apron and put on her fancy linen dress with the lace collar, and soon everyone would be in a jolly mood- dancing to the fiddles and spoons up above and squeaking with joy and happiness.

The Souris family lived a modest, but happy life, under the floorboards of the Dubois homestead in Grand Pré in 1755. The small Acadian village was thriving, full of hard-working, honest folks, who took pride in their work and in their families.

The men worked the fields and built the dykes which held back the mighty tides of the Bay of Fundy, creating some of the most fertile coastal farmland in all of Acadie.

Meanwhile, the women tended the vegetable and herb gardens and made sure that hot, steamy pots of stews and soups hung over the fire-places, ready for the evening meal. The children pitched in too, and took pride in their work and in their lessons.

onsieur Dubois was the village blacksmith, where his shop was a hub of activity. He was a strong, burly man, with thick black curls that fell over his forehead when he worked and a beard that the mice always thought would make a lovely nest!

Madame Dubois was small by comparison, but sturdy and able, with a quick laugh, and she grew the best cabbages in all of Acadie. At least the mice thought so! She had long brown hair which she tucked, braided, under her cap when she worked, and her cheeks looked like they had been kissed by summer roses.

There were five Dubois children, three girls and two boys, Amelie, Aislin, Alisse, Andre and Armand. They helped their Mama and Papa with the chores, and also learned how to write their names on slates and count cobs of corn.

Cecile Souris and her mouse family loved listening to the cheerful sounds of the Dubois family! But one day, the noises upstairs changed, and Cecile knew something was wrong in Acadie. She didn't hear the heavy footsteps of Monsieur Dubois' wooden sabots at the end of the long day. She didn't hear the sounds of a bustling family or squealing children. Instead, all was quiet.

The mice were curious. They peeped out of their mousehole and saw that the kitchen was empty. The floor, which was usually spotless, was still strewn with the remains from the mid-day lunch. And then, they heard the thumping sound coming from outside.

"What's that noise?" asked Etienne, frightened. "Let's go and see," said Cecile, taking her brother's hand. The mice squeezed under the front door and froze, as they felt the vibration of the earth, while soldiers in heavy boots marched over the meadows of their beloved Grand Pré, speaking in a tongue unknown to the mice.

9

The night noises sounded familiar enough. The chickadees sang from the branches of the apple trees, the breezes danced over the wild flowers and the leaves rustled in the night air. But something wasn't quite right, and Papa Souris was determined to find out what it was.

He warned his family to stay behind, then scampered wearily over to the church, without looking back.

Mama Souris, Cecile and little Etienne huddled together, gaining strength from each other's warm soft fur.

Then they heard something. They heard the Dubois family running home, but something was wrong. Madame Dubois was stumbling and weeping, and the children, who were usually rambunctious and playful, were clinging to each other, looking quiet and bewildered.

Cecile started to count, as she had learned in her lessons from under the kitchen table, "One, two, three. Where are Armand and André? Where is Monsieur Dubois?" she wondered.

"And where is Papa Souris?"

Mama Souris hurried Cecile and Etienne down the mousehole, to their quarters below. She smelled the worry in the air, and soon nobody was even thinking about supper anymore. They were too frightened.

The days after that were long and sombre. The men and boys were gathered within the grounds of the church. The anvil in the village blacksmith shop lay quiet and the forge was stone cold. The dykes beckoned and the cows bellowed in the fields of Grand Pré. The whole town stood still, watching and waiting.

Women, children and little mice shivered, with fear and foreboding, and even the fires in the fireplaces of the cozy village homes could not warm their hearts. So the mice just nibbled whatever tidbits of roots, berries and kernels they could find, and they too watched and waited.

The beaches on the Acadian shore were now filled with soldiers shouting orders and boats coming in and out with the tides. When the day finally arrived and the vessels were ready, the women and children were ordered to wait on the beach. The mice gathered their meagre belongings and scurried, unnoticed, along the path to the shoreline, following the scent of the sea.

"If the Dubois family is leaving their Grand Pré home," said Mama Souris, with a new strength in her voice, "We will not abandon them!"

The Acadians, with the mice scurrying about underfoot, waited on the cold, muddy beach until the tide made its way to the shore. Beyond the Minas Basin was the comforting sight of Cape Blomidon, where the Mi'kmaq chief, Glooscap, silently watched. It was then that the families were pushed onto the boats, crying and clinging to each other. As the last of the Dubois children walked toward the boat, little Amelie Dubois grabbed a rock from the beach and clenched it tightly in her fist. Cecile Souris, not far behind, watched her, and scooped a few grains of sand and a shell into her front paw too.

The boat was rocky, cold and scary. The mice had never been near the water before, for fear of shore birds and owls. Now they huddled under the bench, their tails quivering, beneath the shivering Madame Dubois and the three girls. Monsieur Dubois, Armand, Andre and Papa Souris were on another boat, bobbing far ahead, and they all prayed that they would end up on the same faraway shores.

The mouths of the Dubois and Souris families were parched and dry, and water was scarce, but no one complained. With the force of their Acadian spirit, they sang soft melodies. It reminded Cecile of the Saturday night soirées back in their warm, comfortable home, but this time, there was no foot stomping. No fiddles or spoons. Just the sound of the waves and the calling of the gulls.

When the boat finally docked, the mice could barely walk, but they couldn't wait to get off the boat onto dry land. They scurried after the feet of the Dubois family and sniffed the air. It was warm and moist and smelled of magnolia flowers. Pelicans swooped over the water, looking for fish or scraps. Along the shore, where the cypress trees boldly beckoned, several boats rested, full of Acadians who had been deported from their homes. There were even a few other mouse families running amongst the feet and dirt, already searching for food.

A boat full of men and boys was already docked. The children and mice could barely contain themselves as they saw a big, burly man with a bedraggled black beard emerge from the boat with his two sons. Papa Souris limped after them, his whiskers drooping from the heat and hunger.

When everyone laid eyes on each other, they cried with joy and hugged one another. "Papa," cried Cecile, "I'm so happy to see you!" All of a sudden, nothing else in the world mattered but being together again.

Grand Pré seemed very far away. This new land may be their future, but they carried the dykes, the marshes and rolling hills of Acadie in their hearts, like the pebble and beach sand from home in their pockets.

Eventually, some of the families made their homes in the new land. Some wandered, as far as Louisiana. They fished for shrimp and grew crops of sweet potato and sugar cane. The mice settled under the floorboards of the Dubois family's new home, and scavenged for strange spicy crumbs and rice. Their new beds were made from soft cotton fibres, unlike the hay they had slept on in Acadie. The Dubois family continued to work hard and honest lives, often wondering, like the mice, why they had to leave their land and their homes to start all over again, and determined to return one day to the land of their hearts and heritage, Grand Pré.

Years later, Cecile sat under the kitchen table, nibbling a bit of okra and licking her whiskers, when she noticed a bare foot beginning to tap. Then she heard stamping and the sound of a fiddle and a banjo and some spoons. She heard laughter and music, and a familiar *joie de vivre*. She closed her eyes and she could see the hills of Grand Pré in her little mind. She could still smell the fresh sea scent of the Bay of Fundy and she could see the clover blowing across the meadow.

A tear fell down her furry face, but she smiled, proud of who she was and her Acadian roots, knowing that some day she would tell her children all about her home under the floorboards of the Dubois household, in the village of Grand Pré.

ut for now, Cecile picked up her cotton skirt, kicked off her shoes, and danced!

A BRIEF HISTORY OF THE ACADIANS

The French founded the historic village of Grand Pré, on the Minas Basin, in Nova Scotia in about 1675. It served as one of the chief settlements of Acadia and lies between the towns of Wolfville and Windsor. The name, Grand Pré, means "large meadow" in French.

Following the Queen Anne's War in 1713, the French gave Acadia to the English with the Treaty of Utrecht. The Acadians, however, remained loyal to the French and kept close ties with the native Mi'kmaqs. In 1755, the Acadians made a final refusal of the British oath of allegiance to the King. As a result, a force of New England colonial troops gathered up the inhabitants of Grand Pré and other Acadian communities, from Port Royal to New Brunswick, and deported them to American colonies along the Atlantic coast. (Many mice families are said to have also made the voyage!). The majority of Acadians found themselves in what is now known as Massachusetts, Connecticut, Rhode Island, New York, Pennsylvania, New Jersey, Maryland, Delaware, Virginia, North Carolina, South Carolina and Georgia, although some ended up as far away as French Guyana.

Many Acadians were refused entry at their destination points and were sent on a long voyage to England, where they were imprisoned until 1763, when they were sent to France. Some of these Acadians eventually emigrated to Louisiana.

After enduring much hardship, some of the exiled Acadians along the eastern seaboard made their way back to Acadia and lived in peace after the signing of the Treaty of Paris in 1763. Others migrated westward to Louisiana, a former French colony. Descendants of these Acadians are known as Cajuns.

A replica of the church in Grand Pré was dedicated in 1922 and is now a museum. Acadia is best known as the poetic name of Nova Scotia, the famous setting for Henry Wadsworth Longfellow's romantic poem, "Evangeline."

In the summer of 2004, the *Congrès Mondial Acadien* was held in Nova Scotia to bring together Acadians from all over the world to celebrate their heritage.

Produced & Published by
DPG: DERY PUBLISHING GROUP
(A Division of 3643433 Canada Inc.)
1500 Notre Dame
Lachine, Québec, Canada, H8S 2E3
Tel. 514.639.5575
www.derygroup.com

Printed by Dery Printing
Design & Layout by MPR Communications

Roger Déry, President and Publisher
Jasmine Brooks, Editor
Design Team:
Denis Bélanger, Zara Godarzi,
Natacha Lavigne, Amanda Foster

ISBN# 2-9808177-2-4

Printed in Canada.

Fiddles & Spoons: Journey of an Acadian Mouse / Hope-Simpson, Lila.
Text Copyright 2004 by Lila Hope-Simpson
Illustrations Copyright 2004 by Doretta Groenendyk.

Summary: Cecile Souris and her mouse family accompany the Acadians as they are deported from
their beloved Grand Pré in 1755.
Historic Fiction. Story Time.

The book was designed in Quark XPress, with type set in
15 point Goudy regular

Dery Publishing Group supports multiculturalism and the arts!
Visit us at www. derygroup.com
To order additional copies, please contact the publisher directly.
info@mprcommunication.com
or visit

www.fiddlesandspoons.com

The Author

Lila Hope-Simpson is a writer and Early Childhood Educator. She loves going for walks in the meadows of Grand Pré and watching the tides on Evangeline Beach. Lila lives in Wolfville, Nova Scotia, with her husband, Ian, who is a blacksmith. She has three children, Rudi, Jasmine and Natasha, along with an active mouse family living underneath her floorboards.

The Illustrator

Doretta Groenendyk paints from her home in Canning, Nova Scotia. She and her family, David, Izra and Reilly often bicycle on the dykes near Grand Pré, their favourite Acadian site.

Author and Illustrator photos by Ian Hope-Simpson